The Golden Disk
DISCARD

Story by
William Bell

Illustrations by
Don Kilby

Doubleday Canada Limited

For Qi-meng

Canadian Cataloguing in Publication Data

Bell, William, 1945–
     The golden disk
Hardcover ISBN 0-385-25441-5; paperback ISBN 0-385-25672-8
I. Kilby, Don. II. Title.
PS8553.E4568G6 1994 jC813'.54 C94-930812-9
PZ7.B45G0 1994

Design by Terry O Communications
Calligraphy by Ting-xing Ye
Thanks to model Vivienne Tai
   and her mother, Katie Tai
Printed and bound in Hong Kong

Published in Canada by
Doubleday Canada Limited
105 Bond Street
Toronto, Ontario
M5B 1Y3

*Thanks to John Pearce, Maggie Reeves, Helen Mah and Don Kilby
for their help in the making of this book. And, as always,
a special thanks to Ting-xing Ye for encouragement and support.*

A note on punctuation: Ming-yue's name is pronounced *meeng-yueh*; and the "q" in "Chong-qing" is pronounced as the first two letters in "church."

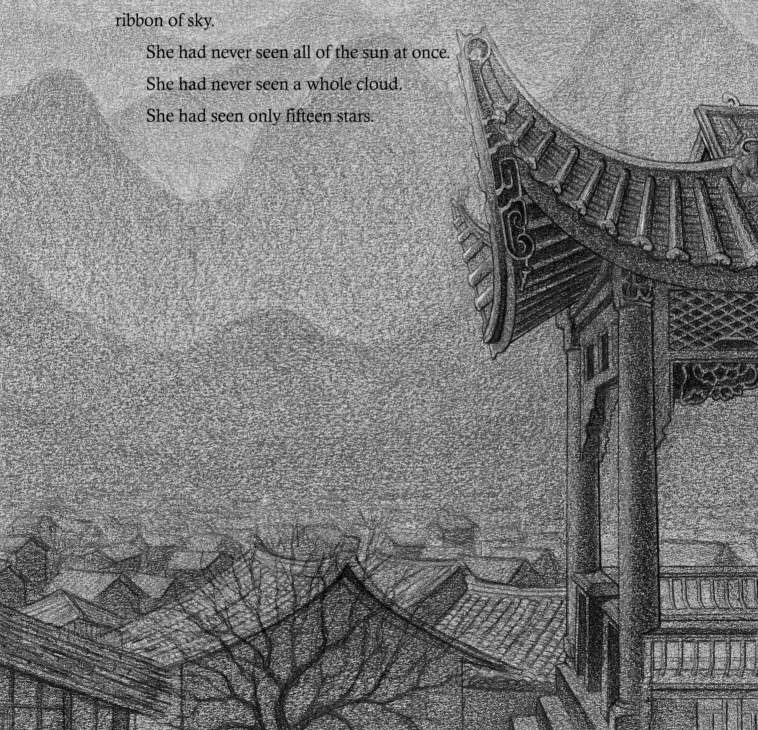

Deep in the blue mountains of China, in an ancient city called Chong-qing, lived a little girl named Ming-yue. Her home was at the farthest end of the longest, twistiest, narrowest, darkest lane in the whole city.

The buildings on each side of the lane towered so high that when Ming-yue looked up she could see only a thin ribbon of sky.

She had never seen all of the sun at once.

She had never seen a whole cloud.

She had seen only fifteen stars.

One cold, clear night in February, when her mother and father, aunties and uncles, grandparents and cousins, and all their friends were eating and drinking to celebrate the New Year, Ming-yue decided to take a walk.

"I'm a big girl, now," she said to herself, "and, since it's New Year's holiday, I'm one year older. I've never been all the way to the other end of our lane. So it's time to see the world!"

And she pulled on her new cotton-padded coat and set out.

Ming-yue followed the many ups and downs and turns of the longest, twistiest, narrowest, darkest lane in Chong-qing. Soon her feet hurt and she was weary, but she was determined to get to the end. After a long, long time she found herself in a quiet square.

Ming-yue noticed right away that the square was not as dark and gloomy as the lane, but seemed washed with gold light. She looked up into a night sky that was much, much wider than a ribbon – and there, above the buildings, was a huge, golden disk!

It seemed so enormous and so close that Ming-yue reached out her hand to touch it. But stretch her arms as she might, wiggle her little fingers as she would, she couldn't quite reach the golden disk.

Ming-yue crouched down to rest her tired legs and stared at the wondrous golden light.

"Maybe it's a ball," she thought, "and it rolled down out of the mountains and got stuck here on the tops of the buildings, and – *Bu, bu, bu!* (which means 'No, no, no!' in Chinese). That can't be true! A ball would have bounced away when it bumped into the buildings."

Ming-yue thought harder. "I know! It's a gold button, lost by the goddess Nü Wa when she was sewing the sky! *Bu, bu, bu!* That can't be true! Nü Wa would never have been so careless."

"Or," she exclaimed, "maybe it's a peach, fallen from the birthday banquet table of Queen Mother of the West and – *Bu, bu, bu!* That can't be true! The Monkey King stole those peaches and hid them in a cave on the Mountain of Flowers and Fruit."

Pressing her fingers to her temples, Ming-yue thought as hard as she could, so hard that her head began to hurt. "Ah," she said after a long moment, "a duck egg! *Bu, bu, bu!* That can't be true! Eggs have shells and they're not round, they're … egg-shaped."

Ming-yue sighed a weary sigh, gazing up at the magnificent golden disk for a long time, making guesses and saying to herself, "*Bu, bu, bu!* That can't be true!" At length she grew tired of thinking and turned into the dark lane, toward home.

When she pushed open her door she found her mother and father, aunties and uncles, grandparents and cousins, and all their friends still celebrating the New Year. After saying good night to each of them, she climbed wearily into the sleeping loft, wriggled deep under her quilt, and went to sleep.

The next morning, after she had eaten her rice gruel and drunk her boiled milk with sugar, Ming-yue filled her pockets with New Year's treats, dashed outside and scampered down the longest, twistiest, narrowest and darkest lane in the city to the square. She looked up, hoping to see the golden disk, but instead she saw dull grey clouds that seemed to hang on the buildings like tattered bedding.

How disappointed she was!

"Where is the disk?" she said to herself. "Did someone steal it? *Bu, bu, bu!* It was much too big to carry.

"Did it melt? *Bu, bu, bu!* Last night it was too chilly.

"Did it roll away during the night? Well ... maybe," she thought. "But where?"

"Do you have something to eat for a poor old man?" came a voice from across the square.

Ming-yue peered into the shadow of an alley and saw an old beggar sitting on a low, three-legged stool. He was wearing ragged, black peasant's clothing and he held out a wooden bowl as she approached.

"Good morning, Uncle," Ming-yue said, remembering her manners. "And happy New Year." She took from her jacket pocket the sweet, glutinous rice balls wrapped in banana leaves that she had brought with her, and placed them in the old man's bowl.

"Please, Uncle, last night I saw a golden disk in the sky. Can you tell me what it was and where it has gone?"

"As it happens, I do know what you saw," he answered in a dry, quiet voice. "And since you are a polite child and a generous one, I am willing to share my secret with you. But, please, join me," he added, holding out his bowl.

Ming-yue refused his offer politely three times before he continued. "I have seen it and yearned for it countless times myself. It's the biggest dumpling under heaven, stuffed fat with the whitest sugar, the sweetest fruit, the nuttiest nuts and the most deliciously aromatic spices. And if you could pull that lovely dumpling out of the sky and break it into pieces, it would feed all of Chong-qing for a year!"

The old beggar smacked his lips as he swallowed the last of the snack Ming-yue had given him. "Now, luckily, it has not gone anywhere. It is stored away during the day, behind the clouds."

"Thank you, Uncle," Ming-yue said, taking her leave. As she trudged home she thought about what the beggar had told her.

"*Bu, bu, bu!* That can't be true!" she said to herself. "The golden disk I saw wasn't a ball, or a button, or a peach, or an egg – or a dumpling. It must be something else. But what?"

Ming-yue sat down to rest on the front step of a tiny shop. Just then the merchant came out the door, struggling with a large bundle of clothing. She was a thin woman with stooped shoulders, but she had a kindly face. Ming-yue jumped up and helped her carry the bundle to the wash-basin that stood beside the steps.

"Hello Auntie," said Ming-yue. "And happy New Year. Do you mind if I rest here for a minute? I have walked a long way."

"Please join me," replied the woman, sitting down herself. "I'm tired, too."

Ming-yue decided to tell her all about the golden disk. She ended by asking, "Auntie, can you tell me what I saw and where it has gone?"

The merchant, who had fallen on hard times and was deeply in debt, sighed a long, long sigh. "Ah, it happens that I know the answer to your question, young miss," she said. "And since you are a helpful little girl, I am willing to share my secret with you. What you saw in the sky was a great coin of purest, gleaming gold. And if you could only pluck it from the sky and break it into pieces, all of Chong-qing would be rich!" As the merchant spoke, her eyes grew bright, and she rubbed her thin hands together.

"But where has it gone?" Ming-yue asked.

"Oh, it is still there! During the day it is hidden and hoarded so that we cannot see it."

After she had thanked the merchant and started on her way again, Ming-yue whispered to herself, "*Bu, bu, bu!* That can't be true! What I saw wasn't a ball, or a button, or a peach, or an egg, or a dumpling – or a coin. But what was it?"

After a while, Ming-yue met her cousin, a university student who was home for the New Year's holiday but was nevertheless burdened with books. Even though he lived in a large family, her cousin always seemed so sad and lonely that everyone called him Mopey. As he passed her in the lane he nodded his head and mumbled a greeting, dropping two or three of his books as he spoke. Ming-yue scooped up the books, brushing the dirt from them with her handkerchief, and returned them to Mopey.

"Please, Cousin," she said. "You have studied a great deal and you must know more than a merchant or a beggar."

"You are too kind," the young man sniffed.

"Can you answer a question for me?" Ming-yue continued. And she went on to describe the huge golden disk she had seen in the wide night sky over the square.

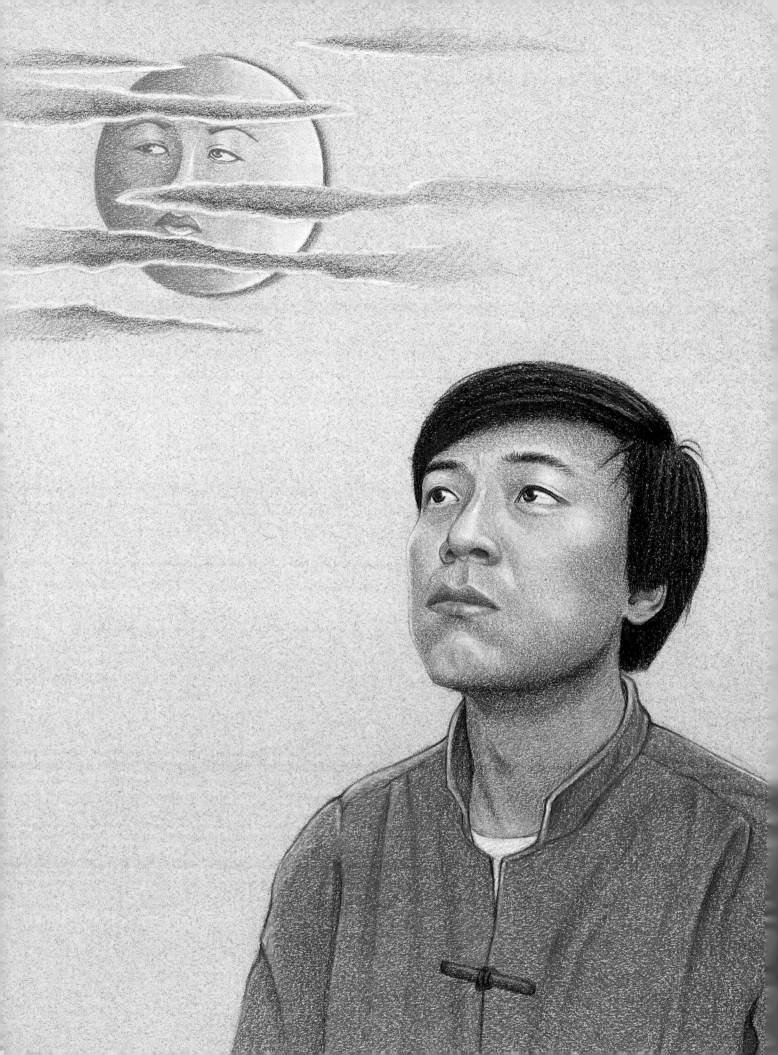

"Ah," her cousin said sadly. "As it happens, I know the answer to your question. And because you are my cousin and helped me with my books, I will share my secret with you. What you saw is the face of a beautiful woman, so distant you cannot make out her delicate features. She is as radiant as gold but as cold as stone. There is no use trying to talk to her for she is cruel and aloof."

"But she is not there today," Ming-yue said. "Where has she gone?"

"During the day she retires to her room to make up her face," her cousin replied. "And she will never, ever come down from the sky."

As Ming-yue watched Mopey wend his way along the lane she said to herself, "*Bu, bu, bu!* That can't be true! It wasn't a ball or a peach or a button or an egg, and it wasn't a dumpling or a coin – or a woman's face. Oh!" she exclaimed, exasperated, "I know what it isn't. I want to know what it is!"

That night Ming-yue was far too tired to go out again, but the following evening, full of hope, she pulled on her new padded coat. The long, twisty lane was even darker than usual, but she was a big girl and she was not afraid. When she reached the square she cast her eyes upwards to see the golden disk.

It wasn't there!

That day it had been very cloudy, and now Ming-yue could see only a blank, black sky. "It must be gone forever!" she cried. How sad and gloomy she was as she trudged slowly home.

"Why so gloomy, Little Sister?" her father asked her when she pushed open the door. "Tonight is the Lantern Festival! Cheer up!"

Her mother and father were making lanterns out of rice paper and slim sticks of bamboo. Tonight everyone in the neighborhood would have a lantern. They would put candles inside them, making the delicate paper glow warmly. The children's lanterns would be shaped like the animals of the zodiac – tigers, dragons, rabbits and monkeys – and placed on wheels so that the children could pull the glowing lanterns along behind them.

Usually, Ming-yue loved the festival. For hours on end, she would watch the lights bob and float up and down the lane. But she felt she would not enjoy it this year.

She pulled herself wearily up onto a chair. "Mom and Dad," she said, "may I ask you something?" And she went on to describe the huge, golden disk, and how she had been trying so hard to find out what it was. And when she told them it was gone, tears trickled from her eyes.

"Well, well, well," said Ming-yue's mother. "It so happens that your Dad and I know the answer to your questions, and because we love you, we will tell you a secret."

"Come and look," said her father, taking a newly made lantern from the shelf above the table. It was a brilliant crimson globe, trimmed with gold paper. He picked up his writing brush and wrote a word on the delicate lantern.

"Now," he said, "this word,

means 'sun', and this one,

means 'moon.'"

Forgetting her manners and interrupting her father, Ming-yue asked excitedly, "What's a 'moon?'"

"Look here," her father went on, smiling at Ming-yue's enthusiasm. "When you put these two words, 'sun' and 'moon' together, like this,

you get a new word, 'bright.'

"Now we write this word again,

which means—"

"Sun!" Ming-yue interrupted again. "*Bu, bu, bu!* That isn't true! It means 'moon.' But what's a moon?"

"Be patient, Little Sister. These two words,

form your name: 'Bright moon.'"